SNOWMEN AT WORK

Caralyn Buehner

pictures by

Mark Buehner

Dial Books for Young Readers  an imprint of Penguin Group (USA) Inc.

One night I made a snowman,
Then went inside to sleep,
And when I woke, I saw more snow
Had fallen soft and deep.

I went outside to shovel
But I saw the walks were clear;
No one else was outside but
My snowman standing near.

Was he the one who shoveled, with a snowman shoveling crew?
Could it be I just don't see that snowmen have jobs too?

The dentist might drill bits of coal
To fix a snowman's smile;
A little brush and polish
Sends the snowman home in style!

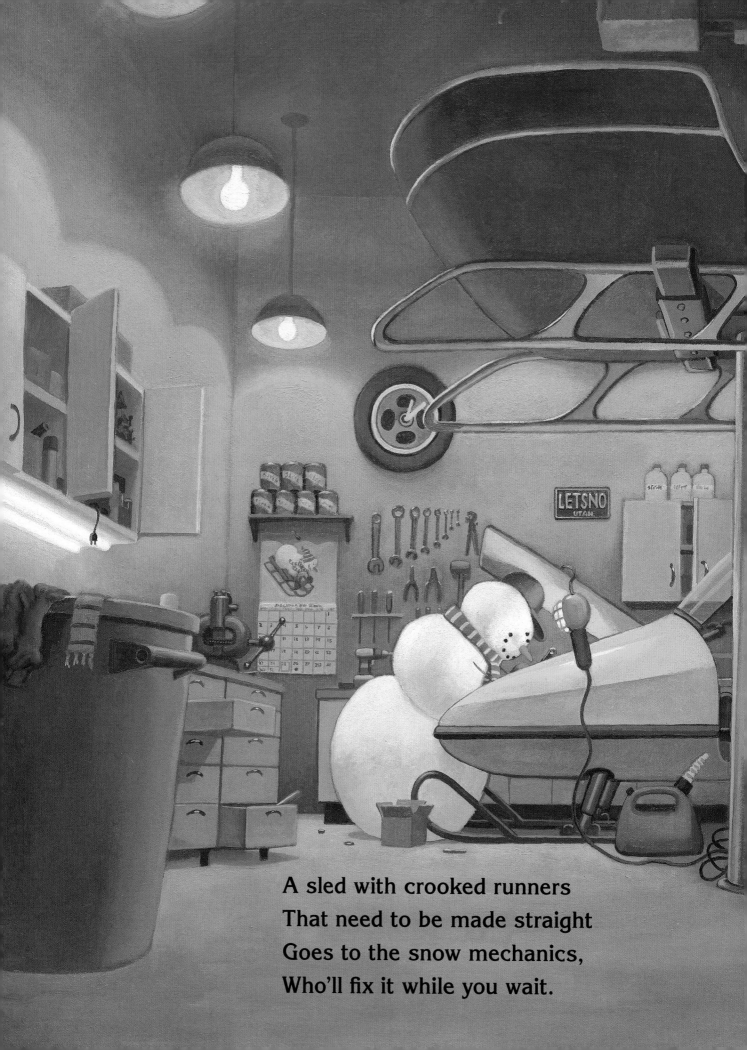

A sled with crooked runners
That need to be made straight
Goes to the snow mechanics,
Who'll fix it while you wait.

The grocer stocks his shelves
With foods that snowmen love to eat:
Frozen peas and Frosty Flakes,
And ice cream for a treat!

Snow children beg their mothers
To go in the snow pet store.
The pet store owner has snow pups,
A coldfish tank, and more.

The baker spreads sweet icing
Onto every frozen bun;
There's frosted cake and ice-cold rolls,
Enough for everyone!

The teachers teach snow children
To count snowflakes one by one,
And how to spell ANTARCTICA,
REFRIGERATE, and FUN.

There might be snow magicians
Who do tricks for their career;
They pull snow rabbits out of hats
Or make them disappear.

If your snow cat is stuck
And there's no way to get it down,
Just call the firefighters—
They're the bravest folks in town!

The story-time librarian
Reads tales from days of yore:
How brave snow knights defend the right,
While mighty dragons roar!

A birthday celebration means a party is in store.
The pizza man delivers frozen pizza to your door.

The factory workers carefully
Assemble jolly toys,
Knowing that they're bringing smiles
To snow girls and snow boys.

The big rig's lights glow brightly
While the tires spin round and round;
The snow truck driver hauls a load
Of frozen goods to town.

My snowman really *might* have
Shoveled, and I never knew
That all around us snowmen
Have a lot of work to do!

For Joy

Readers, see if you can find a cat, a rabbit, a Tyrannosaurus rex, and a mouse in each painting. (The key is on the underside of the book jacket.)

DIAL BOOKS FOR YOUNG READERS • A division of Penguin Young Readers Group • Published by The Penguin Group • Penguin Group (USA) Inc., 375 Hudson Street, New York, NY 10014, U.S.A. • Penguin Group (Canada), 90 Eglinton Avenue East, Suite 700, Toronto, Ontario, Canada M4P 2Y3 (a division of Pearson Penguin Canada Inc.) • Penguin Books Ltd, 80 Strand, London WC2R 0RL, England • Penguin Ireland, 25 St. Stephen's Green, Dublin 2, Ireland (a division of Penguin Books Ltd) • Penguin Group (Australia), 250 Camberwell Road, Camberwell, Victoria 3124, Australia (a division of Pearson Australia Group Pty Ltd) •Penguin Books India Pvt Ltd, 11 Community Centre, Panchsheel Park, New Delhi - 110 017, India • Penguin Group (NZ), 67 Apollo Drive, Rosedale, Auckland 0632, New Zealand (a division of Pearson New Zealand Ltd) • Penguin Books (South Africa) (Pty) Ltd, 24 Sturdee Avenue, Rosebank, Johannesburg 2196, South Africa • Penguin Books Ltd, Registered Offices: 80 Strand, London WC2R 0RL, England • Text copyright © 2012 by Caralyn Buehner • Pictures copyright © 2012 by Mark Buehner • All rights reserved. No part of this book may be reproduced, scanned, or distributed in any printed or electronic form without permission. Please do not participate in or encourage piracy of copyrighted materials in violation of the author's rights. Purchase only authorized editions. •The publisher does not have any control over and does not assume any responsibility for author or third-party websites or their content. •Designed by Lily Malcom
Text set in ITC Korinna •Manufactured in China on acid-free paper • 10 9 8 7 6 5 4 3 2
Library of Congress Cataloging-in-Publication Data • Buehner, Caralyn. • Snowmen at work / Caralyn Buehner ; pictures by Mark Buehner. • p. cm. • Summary: When winter sidewalks seem to have been mysteriously shoveled, a child wonders if snowmen are magic and have nighttime jobs while the people sleep. Includes hidden pictures. • ISBN 978-0-8037-3579-8 (hardcover) • [1. Stories in rhyme. 2. Snowmen—Fiction. 3. Picture puzzles.] I. Buehner, Mark, ill. II. Title. • PZ8.3.B865Suw 2012 • [E]—dc23 • 2011051648

The art was prepared with oil paints over acrylics.